LOST GIRLS GO EVERYWHERE

A Collection of Poetry & Prose

AZZURRA NOX

Dedicated to all the lost girls. You will find your path between the heartbreak and hopes that fuel your dreams. Never give up.

CONTENTS

PART I

POETRY

FIRST DATE

I don't think any man
Has ever slipped a
rape whistle, pocket-knife, and
taser into their handbags
Hoping they wouldn't have to use them
On their first date.

I don't think any man
Has ever had to grip the handle of a car
Wondering if their date is actually
Driving to the movies,
Instead of a remote location
Readying yourself to jump out of a
moving car to save yourself –
But also endangering yourself.

I don't think any man
Has ever had to pick up their pace
Walking a parking lot at night
Never having the luxury
Of a leisure stroll
Unable to breathe in the summer air
Because you're too focused on
the footsteps behind you

And struggling between the fight or flight.

I don't think any man
Has ever been in the position
Of being afraid to insult their partner
Thinking that maybe this person
Could kill them if they felt wronged.

I don't think any man
Has had labored breaths
From the weight of our fear
and dread
Where we're constantly on high alert
No place is safe for us
Everyplace is a danger zone.

I don't think any man
Has ever had to worry about
being a target
Even when you're keeping yourself safe
They will judge your clothes
And say that you were asking for it.

GOODBYE, MELODY

We crowded around the mirror
Painting our lips sinful red
We got drunk on Bailey's
Because we were young and dumb

With Red Hot Chili Peppers on repeat
We daydreamed of Hollywood
And all the things we would become
Model, actress, triple threat superstar

Even then a part of me knew
That all our dreams would only remain
Dreams
Something to sigh over when we were older

But then I left for Hollywood
Without you
I was too old for frivolous dreams
And didn't try to become
Any of those things I wished I could be
All those things we were certain we
could achieve

When they told me that you died

I already knew why before being told
All I asked was, "How?"
Because even at seventeen your gaze
Held a brokenness to it
That gave me insight into your future

I just wish that my intuition had been wrong
That I could be walking the Walk of Fame with you
Bathing in the waters of the Pacific Ocean together
Getting drunk in Griffith Park
Falling in love with movie stars

Although I'm often tempted to join you
I feel the burden of having to live
For the both of us
Striving to live and love
Like you can no longer do
Even if sometimes, I wish I could let go
Because living without you has become
A punishment I always wished I didn't have to endure.

RUNNER-UP

Whenever I watch a beauty pageant
I never relate with the winner
But rather with the almost queen
So close to wearing the tiara
Like her,
I'm like that hapless poker player
Always holding the winning card too late.

STARRY EYES

Your neglect has managed to
Burst my heart into so many tiny pieces
That I was unable to recover all
The love that I bled out

I listen to your old songs about me
In hopes that I can feel that rush
I felt the first time that our eyes locked
Nothing could give me more joy
Than to *feel*

Remember when we had starry eyes
Our lips spoke poetry in every kiss
Remember when we had starry eyes
Our limbs resonated with music in every caress

I had a Kate Moss smile
Your nonchalance was so very James Dean
I read all the books you loved
If only to see the world from your perspective

My whole essence breathed you into me
I've never been the same again
There's a hole in my chest

Where all my love for you resided

Remember when we had starry eyes
Our lips spoke poetry in every kiss
Remember when we had starry eyes
Our limbs resonated with music in every caress

What kills me
Is that I remember everything about our days
Together
What kills me
Is that I can't recreate that feeling of starry eyes
With anyone else.

EARTHQUAKE

The first time the earth shook beneath my feet
I merely thought that the storm in my heart
Had finally become a tangible thing
And not something I suffer
On my own.

INSOMNIAC

Some nights I wish I could simply sleep soundly
Clutching nothing but your photo
But some nights
The fact that you're only a photograph for me
Now
Is enough to keep me up all night.

WE ARE GODS

Ask any Sicilian and they will tell you
That they're Gods
That is why they refuse
To embrace the future
And cling to the past
Because descendants of Apollo
Have no place in modern life
The Greek theatres are crumbling
And yet they hold unto their masks
Reciting Antigone

Ask any Sicilian and they will tell you
That cyclops live on Etna
And that any woman could be
The daughter of Medusa
Ready to punish men
For their preying eyes
Condemning them to a
Lifetime of silence
Looking out out of stone pupils

Ask any Sicilian and they will tell you
We're still a Greek colony
That we're unable to accept

The Catholic God
Because we used to be Gods
We are Gods
Only no longer worshiped.

BAD HABIT

I'm like a smoker
In need of a cigarette
I need you, even if
I know you're detrimental
To my health

But the rush you give me
Is worth more
Than saving myself.

BOLD

What I learned from Icarus
Wasn't that he fell from the sky
But that for a moment
He was exploding with joy
For having reached the sun.

I yearn to be that fearless.

AGEISM IS FASCISM

Stop seeing my body as a time bomb
Youth is overrated
I don't wish to erase
The memories from my face
How will I know that I gained
Any knowledge
If I remove the culprits?

Stop seeing my body as a time bomb
That I'll become useless
Once I'm incapable of housing a baby
In my womb
What if I never desired to house
Anything in my body
But art?

My body isn't a time bomb.
It's a book of unwritten poems.

LOVE LOST TO ROUTINE

There was a time when love hung upon your tongue
I remember when you'd look at me with that gaze
That seemed to whisper a thousand I love yous
Now there's only a fastidious indifference
Spring has left us for awhile
And we've settled into the most barren winters
I wish I could cut my chest open
Rip my heart from my ribcage
Because I often wonder if it has gone dead
Or if it simply has ceased beating for you
All I can think of is passionate loves
The sort that make you tear your hair
The ones where every kiss feels like your first
This mediocre routine affection has atrophied
My emotions
I want more
And yet you say that we are lucky
That years together stand for something
Commitment and loyalty
But my heart is disloyal
It yearns for stolen kisses
I often wonder if we lie to ourselves
Domesticity is the tomb of love
And ours has long been buried.

SUPERNOVA

Summers spent with sticky fingers
And cotton candy kisses
The Luna Park was our campground
Of our young love
Dancing to terrible music on repeat
Drinking rum and coke
You were the patron saint of vice
Blowing smoke rings and
Your hand in my hair
Whenever I'd suck your cock
Trying to be edgy
Wearing a torn I Love LA top
My lipstick smeared like Harley Quinn
Flying in the night on your motorcycle
The wind in my hair
Feeling free
Stars flowing from our wrists
Instead of blood
We were magical
We were invincible
We were one.

MIDNIGHT SECRET

It's that time of night
Where I shut off my brain
Where I cast out the world
And I am alone
With you.
I purposely never speak of you
Frightened that my eyes will
Light up at your very memory
Too scared
That I won't be able to conceal
The sugared affection in my voice
Were I to utter your name.
My tongue might lie
But my heart cannot.
I've never understood
What you and I are
But whatever we are
Our souls are forever intertwined
I'm the Catherine to your Heathcliff
And we're just as hapless
As Wuthering Heights
It's that time of night
Where I can relive our moments together
As I slowly drift to sleep

With hopes that I'll meet you in my dreams
Because I know that once I'm awake
I will have to be without you
Another day.

FIRST CUTS KILL

I should've known I was set up for heartbreak
The moment my eyes settled upon you
You were a modern Mozart
Wild hair and hands that could create
The most beautiful music
I yearned to be your piano
I wanted to be your favorite song
Maybe if I hadn't been so young
I would've known that you were
A beautiful disaster
I had so much love for you
Just bursting at the seams with affection
I would've given anything to be your girl
But I didn't know what to do
My teenage days were filled with a
Poe-ridden depression
Because I kept trying to make you mine
Always chasing your love
Not knowing that your heart
Was never something I could steal
Facing the world like I had been locked
In Mr. Rochester's attic
Screaming at the injustice
Of being unloved

Not knowing that only some of us
Are meant to be the heroines
While the rest of us are forced to be
The villains
When I finally vomited my heart
Leaving it on your doorstep
You pitied my frailty
Wishing me good luck
But had I been lucky
I never would've met you.

GLOBETROTTER

We kissed in London
We fell in love in Paris
We had our fight fight in Vienna
We made up in Prague
We made love in Barcelona
We promised forever in Berlin
We came undone in Oslo
We died a violent death in Rome.

SAFE HARBOR

Will I ever have that moment
Where I'll become
Someone's safe harbor
I wish to be the port
Someone unloads the secrets
You reveal at 3a.m.
Over cigarettes and coffee
Will I ever have that moment
Where I'll become
Someone's safe harbor
Where the sight of my port
Will bring the greatest relief
After weathering storms
Will I ever have that moment
Before my time runs out?

BEAUTIFUL

He is beautiful
Not because his eyes are like the ocean
Nor because his lips are kissable
He is beautiful

Because he holds my heart
Knowing that it could shatter
If he were to let go
But yet chooses to cradle it

As though it is the most fragile
and precious crystal
Worth holding on to.

OUR LOVE WAS WORTH A MILLION SCARS

Our love was too wild
It burned too bright
Outsiders cautioned us that it wouldn't last
But young love is stubborn
We wanted to defy the stars
We wanted to be immortal
Perhaps we bled an ocean
And maybe we were left impaired
But some loves are worth all the scars
We're left to bear.

THERE'S NO TAMING MY DEMON

I let my thoughts chase me out of the city
He insists on buying me a drink
I wonder what he sees
If he, like all the others, merely sees
A pretty girl with a sad smile
No one will ever understand
The storm that dwells in my heart
Small talk is made for those
Who don't have murderous intentions
Of the soul
My broken heart has been festering for years
I left a love behind on an island
That many only know for
Marlon Brando being a Godfather
I wish there were words to explain
The various nuances of the
Train wreck that I am
These men with gentle smiles
And eager eyes
Can't understand what it's like
To be drinking poison for years
Eventually everyone leaves
Because no one can tame
My demon

Because when I tell them
I'm intense
They think I'm lying
Or when I tell them
I'm crazy
They think I'm being funny
I warn them
And yet
They still look up with blood
In their eyes,
Their expression horrified
By the deep cracks in my heart
That not even San Andrea's Fault
Runs as deep as my pain
I let my thoughts chase me out of the city.

CALIFORNIA WILDFIRE

Our first kiss was in the depths of a
Fetish Room
It was summer, the time of year
For love to blossom like wild daisies
We burned bright and dangerous
A forest fire gone rogue
Suddenly, I felt more daring
Not thinking about tomorrow
The killer of passion
All I wanted to think about
Was how your kisses
Ignited fireworks in me
Exploding into the brightest colors
Whenever we were in the same room
We transformed into a danger zone
Our flames devouring the walls
And although our hearts had
No fire escape to lead us out
We kept on playing Russian roulette
Loading our guns with six bullets
Because death by love
Was ultimately better than
A slow, tedious death.

A DANGER TO HERSELF AND OTHERS

Young girls don't know they're a danger
Not until they first bleed
And their breasts blossom
Pressing polo shirts with their perkiness
It's almost scandalous

Young girls don't know they're a danger
To themselves when they drink
And men wait for them to let down
Their guard
So they can become wolves beneath
Villain sheets

Young girls don't know they're a danger
To others
Men are so convinced
That it's our bodies that make them monsters
Not admitting that
It's our minds that they are truly afraid of.

QUEENS ARE BETTER OFF ALONE

I've dreamed of days where I'd be queen
But I never envisioned a king
Because don't we all know
That a queen without a king
Has always been more powerful
Than what her people ever gave her
Credit for
I want to be a queen
Without a king
So that I can overtake the whole
Fucking castle
I don't believe in sharing my reign.

INCAPABLE OF TAMING THE SHREW

I'm the secret ingredient
To your downfall
My love is fatal
Not made for the fragile

I relish in fires
And add gasoline
To mediocre passions
Just so I can watch them
Blow up

There's a strange satisfaction
In breaking a man
To watch him beg
For your love
Because men have always
Been attracted to danger

It's why the captain
Yearned for Moby Dick
He would've given up
If overtaking it
Were simple

Men love to taste the blood
That flow from their wounds
As I twist my knife into their hearts
Making them feel more alive
Than the day they took their first breath.

CIGARETTE SCREEN

Smoke curls up in the air,
Lingering over me like a phantom.
Dark rooms suggest obtuse shadows.
Beethoven notes vibrate against closed walls.
The smell of wet trees and dirt infiltrates inside
Like a sneaky cat between a half-closed door.
Memories past come briefly to life.
A wet kiss, humid bodies skin to skin.
Dew drops rolling off of balmy limbs.
The smoke swallows the broken images.
Pictures of the past—now only gray smoke
Evaporating into nothingness.
Have another cigarette, light up another
Particle from your youth.
Don't put out the fire—not until it's over.

YOU

You.
Yes, you.
You are the sun
On my rainy days.

You.
Yes, you.
You are the good
On my bad days.

You.
Yes, you.
You are the calm
When I'm the storm.

You.
Yes, you.
You never let go
Even when I'm slipping.

You.
Yes, you.
You are the love
I always dreamed of.

BLOOD REMEMBERS EVEN WHEN YOU DON'T

I left lipstick imprints on your neck
We bathed in rose petals and strawberries
Champagne kisses
You were like a tormented Arthur Rimbaud
All the girls bursting with love for you
But you only had eyes for me
Baby, it wasn't maybe
And I was living free like Carole Lombard
We didn't know we were bound for heartbreak
The young are fearless
Baby, we were crazy
Wrapped in our intoxicating dreams of forever
Chasing each other in the night
Our hearts exploding with possibilities
Sometimes we look back and try to grasp
How we fell apart
But baby, it was never maybe
We're immortal in the blood and memories we left behind.

THE WAY YOU LEFT ME

I housed dreams in my heart
You used razor blades to tear them out.
Hope lingered on my lips
You bit down hard till they bled.
You left me bloody and empty.
In a world that wants us to be whole and pristine.

LATE

I've arrived too late.
You've used up all your love and
outrageous displays of affections on someone else.
So that when Valentine's Day passes by,
There are no flowers or romantic adventures.
You tell me, "I've done this all before—I'm tired."
But you've done nothing with me
For me.
I'm left picking up the crumbs,
cause I've come too late
And someone else has already eaten my cake.

THE LESSONS WE'RE TAUGHT

Men are taught to take what they please
Women are taught to relinquish their treasures with a smile.
It's why women mistake brutality for love
And men believe a woman's body is for them
to seize without consequences.

UNWANTED MEMORIES

I removed your mark from my skin,
They gave me pills to forget.
I begged the stars to stop
spelling your name
But they're cruel,
So I blinded myself instead.
There's peace in darkness.

BROKEN DOLL

Love has treated me
Like a toddler treats
Its toy.
That's why my hair is in tangles
and my limbs are broken.

MARLON BRANDO

He had so much love for me
That it often made him crazy
Yelling from the streets
Like Marlon Brando
Shouting, "Stella!"

He had so much love for me
That he wasn't sure how to suffocate it
Often his mannerisms were crude
Thinking that I owed him
Affection, thinking he were
Marlon Brando and who always
Got the girl

He had so much love for me
That it poisoned him from the inside
Because rejection was seen as disdain
But pity has no place for passion
Nor can a friendship be forced
Into a relationship

Because he wasn't Marlon Brando
And the script I wrote
Didn't cast him as the hero

He merely had a supporting role
I didn't want him at my premiere
Nor did I want him shouting
Beneath my window, "Stella!"
Thinking he were Marlon Brando.

BAD OMEN

I've got so much misfortune that
I'm bathing in my bad omens.

NOBODY'S WIFE

I hate weddings because
They're a reminder of
Something I'll never have
I know that most marriages
End in divorce
And yet I wish
Someone had believed in a
Forever
With me
However brief
But I'm a terrible salesman
Because I couldn't sell you a
Dream.

BEAUTIFUL DISASTER

I knew it was going to be a beautiful disaster,
And yet I pursued him —not caring if I was stepping into the eye of
the tornado.
I wanted him.
He would be mine.
Or....
There was no or.
Just a certainty that my life wouldn't ever be the same without him.

MR. PERFECT

It is those men you think are perfect—that
will do you the most harm.

SCHOOL DANCE WOES

You're sitting on the bleachers wearing a purple velvet dress
You curled your hair and wore new Cover Girl lipgloss
The DJ puts on a slow song—
And you won't know it until it's too late that everyone is dancing
But you.
When you arrive home you cry because your parents ask you why
you were the only one not dancing.
You hadn't noticed in the moment.
From that day you vow to never go to another school dance ever
again.
Too humiliating.
But sometime around Junior year you have a change of heart
and decide to attend Prom.
But when the DJ puts on terrible slow songs
It triggers something in you
You feel sick
So sick that you run outside
The cold air against your cheeks
They freeze your tears
Icicles
When you return
your date asks you where you went
And all you can say is,
"I'm feeling under the weather, I think I'm going to go."

LIVING WITH DEATH AS YOUR LOVER

I'm forever hanging from a thread that's threatening to break
Perpetually dangling my feet into the unknown
Hoping that today won't be the day I fall.

DEPRESSION

Owning a new dress
But not having the enthusiasm to wear it.
A plate full of delicious delicacies
And your stomach flips with dread.
Being told that you are loved
And yet feeling so alone.
Seeing yourself in the mirror
And not recognizing the person staring back at you.

I'M NOT OKAY

My shoulders ache with the burden of carrying so much baggage
I'm tired of being the protagonist of the same tragic love story
No matter which choice I make the outcome is always the same
And yet,
I carry on—pretending that I'm okay
Sometimes, I repeat to myself, "I'm okay," as tears slide down my
face
As I feel my heart implode for the nth time
Believing
That with each repetition it'll stop feeling like a lie
It takes courage to admit that you're a mess
And I'm a coward when it comes to honesty
I'm a pathological liar of white lies
As though lying to myself might make me perceive reality
differently
Or that maybe my lies might just become real
"I'm okay."
But I haven't been okay for a very long time
That I've forgotten how it feels to truly feel alive
I meander through the motions
Fork in hand, shoving food as a means to survive
I'm an actor
I could win an Oscar for the trillion times I've led everyone to
believe

That I'm okay
The few times I've allowed the curtain to fall
Has been met with dismal looks and judgment
"What's wrong?"
Never meant as a question but coming across as an accusation
What's wrong?
Everything
And nothing
I'm not okay
But I don't know how to tell you
Without feeling like I've let you down
So I continue to swallow razorblades
Bleeding dishonest words
"I'm okay."
No one ever wonders why my mouth is so full of blood.

THE PRODIGY

Child prodigies are revered at their peak
As adults people find a perverse satisfaction in watching these now-
grown children flounder
Unable to swim into adulthood because they've spent all their time
being young marvels
Who cares that you could write a symphony at five
If you grew up to be a drunk?
What does it meant to have been the youngest Academy Award
recipient
If you're now homeless and sold your Oscar for heroin?
Why do we celebrate failures
As a means to feel accomplished?

FLIRTING WITH DEATH

I used to flirt with the idea of death
My waking moments felt so unbearable that death
Was my only solution to a permanent sleep
A part of me was hoping that the afterlife would
Prove to be more satisfying, less cynical and cruel
I was sixteen, dressed in melancholy and Doc Martens
No one could understand how my sunny disposition had been
Brutally murdered
I was bleeding black storm clouds
All over the living room floor
I'm sorry I ruined the expensive Oriental rug, mother
It's going to take me a lifetime to repay you
I used to flirt with the idea of death
Until one night, Death plucked me from my bed
And whispered sweet nothings until I was convinced that my time
was up
I couldn't confess the extent of my sadness to anyone
My parents would merely see my sadness as a reflection of
themselves
And I didn't want to let them down
I texted friends heartfelt messages and maybe it's telling of how
much
I censor my own feelings, that suddenly many of them panicked
"Gasp! She used the l-word! And wasn't joking!"

Panicked to the point that one of them came
He was almost too late
But in a string of misfortunes, for once Lady Luck made her
appearance
And as my friend rammed his fingers down my throat
I realized how deceitful Death can be
She makes you believe she's a beautiful muse
When she's nothing more than an ugly hag dressed in designer
clothes
There wasn't anything poetic or romantic in throwing up barbiturates
The acid burning my throat, reminding me that I was still alive and
that death was ugly
How can something so horrid paint itself so pretty?
I used to flirt with the idea of death
'Til the night I almost died and found out how fleeting life really is
And how I should give my love to those that want me to stay
Rather than bestow my adoration to someone who only wants me to
leave.

BEAUTY MARKS

He ran his hands along my body and said, "Have you ever thought
of getting rid of them?"
I was confused, because what he saw as blemishes, I saw as beauty.

MOTHER OF ART

I've grown weary of being made to feel less than
When my childless aunt tells me,
"Melanie is expecting her third child, and she's not even thirty!"
As though we were marathon runners in a race to procreate
Besides, I've been birthing poetry since I was 13
Does anyone see me flaunting?
My children aren't flesh and bone
Tears and stars run through their veins
And will beat a heart until the end of time
Unlike Melanie's mere mortals.

THE QUITTER

I give up
On romantic love
I've spent so much time
Loving people
Who do not love me.
Pouring energy into
People that only
Make me feel alone,
Taken for granted,
Underappreciated,
Broken,
Ugly.
I give up
My body has run out of blood
From cutting myself open
To make room for someone else
I give up
I've been force fed
Humble pie too many times
Dealt with glazed eyes
And groping hands
Swallowed beautiful lies
And vomited ugly truths
I give up

On you
Because I've learned to love
Myself.

BIG WINNER

I'm the lottery ticket
You threw away
Thinking I wasn't the jackpot
Believing that I was worthless
But I had the winning numbers all along
You just never paid attention
Too caught up by
Your other options
Disregarding my potential
Blind to my love
Now you curse Lady Luck
Because someone else
Claimed the prize
When it had always been
Within your reach.

PORTRAIT OF A HAPPY FAMILY

We were never a happy family
No matter how many times you lie to me
And say that we were
Have you forgotten about all the fights?
How sitting down for dinner felt like awaiting death row?
Or how I often excused myself from the table
So that I could hide out in the bathroom
Because I was filled with so much contempt
Over how much hatred seeped from the both of you.
We were never a happy family
Family vacations didn't exist
Because neither of you could stomach each other
Long enough for a holiday
Neither of you spoke fondly of the other
Instead—
You'd both list each others' faults
In screaming accusations that reeked of disdain
We were never a happy family
No matter how many layers of veneer
You slapped upon us to make us appear
Picture perfect.

ONE DAY

I always knew we wouldn't have a lifetime together
I merely wanted one day
So that I could live the rest of my life
With that memory of you.

ALL THAT I WANT

All I ever wanted in life
Was a house by the sea
And you by my side.

WITCH

You tried to burn me at the stake
But I've got the strength
Of one hundred witches
That have come before me.
If I were you
I wouldn't mess with this bitch.

SELF-TALK

Your legs are disgustingly thick, you're never going to have a thigh
gap
You are nothing
How can you always say the wrong thing?
Why can't you be happier?
Why can't you brighten a room like the brightest star, rather than
dimming it like a storm?
How can I be so skinny and yet feel so fat?
STOP!
Be kind.
Please rewind.

GO WEST

Head to Los Angeles they told me
You can reinvent yourself there.
I can forget that I ever swallowed pills
wishing to die.
I can erase that you ever broke my heart
I can be renewed
Upgraded
Resurrected into a green juice drinking
Writer/Model/Actress
Cause in Los Angeles you can be anyone.
I can be someone else
I don't have to be myself.
I don't have to be the girl who almost died because of
You.

DREAMS

In my dreams I'm always laughing
Maybe because I spend so much time
In my waking life crying.

STORM CLOUDS

There's a storm in my heart -
It's going to obliterate everyone.

TWENTY YEARS

Two decades have passed
Since the first time that we met
And yet it still burns the brightest
Out of all the loves my heart has ever
Thump-thump-thumped for
After one hundred days together
You bathed me in one hundred roses in Paris
To celebrate us
Our love had all the ingredients of
Star-crossed couples
Across history
Doomed from the very start
You were my soulmate
And it's a tragedy
Because I can only refer to you
In past tense
When my feelings are still
In Present
I'm incapable of removing
Your photo from my bedside table
Two decades
And yet I still want you to be
The first and last person I see
In my day

You're the one love
I cannot bring myself to see you
Anymore
You're dangerous
Because I get weak knees and breathless
Instead
I keep us trapped in amber
Our younger selves
Perfectly intertwined
Reading poetry and Shakespeare
To each other
Eating chocolates naked in bed
And stealing kisses at a Cure concert
That's how I want to remember us
Sitting in the back of a car
Late at night, eating arancini
Running into the cold night
Waters of the sea
Our lips blue, our kisses salty
You were my soulmate
That's the tragedy
Because you're in the past
And I'm stuck in a present
Without you
You were romance
And you were love
You were lust
And you were affection
You were everything
And I've had to learn to live with
Nothing
When you've been drinking champagne
For so long
It's difficult to settle for beer
My nights end in L.A.
While you're just waking up in London
Two decades and I can still feel

Your lips on my flesh
When it's past midnight
And the world has gone dead
But the memories come alive
Newly minted and clearer to me
Than those acquired only yesterday
Two decades and so many love stories later
And yet
Yes
My heart is still brandished with your name.

NO BLOOD RELATIONS

Family is whoever sticks with you
Even at your worst.

IT'S NOT ME IT'S YOU

Often the actions of others
Lead me to kill my enthusiasm
It's why I seem so dead
I've been silently killing myself
Since seventeen.

THE WANDERER

I've run out of places to call home
Every time, I arrive wide-eyed and willing
Yearning to belong
Pleading for a sense of wholeness
How many places can I run to
Before I've run out of places?
Every new city feels temporary
Every new home feels like a motel
When can I sink my roots in
Or must I always be confined to being a
Potted plant, my scenery forever shifting?
If you slit my veins
Do I bleed red, white, and blue?
Or is my blood red, white, and green?
Each new place offers the promise of a new
Beginning
Maybe this time, this will feel like home, I tell myself every time.
But month pass, and then the cold realization sinks in
Freezing my optimism –
I'm forever a stranger in a strange place.
Is home pasts with ricotta? Is it almond cookies made using my
Nonno's recipe?
Is home Friday night horror movies and popcorn? Is it Crystal Pepsi
and Ranch Doritos?

Home
A certainty for many
A question for me.
When will the search end?
Home –
Maybe I long for a place that doesn't exist.

PART II

MY BAD ROMANCE
PROSE

THE PIANIST

Maybe if I had met him when I was older, I would've known that he was a beautiful disaster and that our so-called love was merely a one-sided obsession. But when you're thirteen and you meet an older boy (he was seventeen at the time) with long, black hair who plays Beethoven in a way that makes your heart fall apart, well….you can't help but feel like he's the one.

I was a fellow pianist, such as him (although not quite as talented) and so that already made me feel as though we had something in common. So it was natural for me to suggest that he'd give me some tutoring lessons (which he had accepted to). My thirteen-years-old heart beat so fast you'd think I was close to a coronary. I was gonna be the first teenager to die of a burst-from-happiness heart.

Sadly, that happiness was very short lived.

Fast forward to when I'm seventeen. The Pianist and I are now not only friends, but I've managed to become a staple in his household. We've done Easter plays together, our families have spent holidays together, and we even planted a cactus together, my heart expanding every year when it'd bloom flowers, as though it were some proof of our unwavering love. But I was growing increasingly frustrated with my limited friend label. I wanted more. I wanted a mad love, stolen kisses, and passionate summer nights. I wanted ice cream dates, movie dates, and gazing at the stars.

Then his twenty-first birthday came around and for the first time that I had ever known him he was having a party.

"I hope you can make it tonight," he told me, his dark eyes shining with a secret. "I've got something I want to tell you."

My brain went through all the various scenarios of what he could possibly be wanting to tell me. Of course, the curse of being in love is that you're always hopeful, and so I spent the day listening to a shitty love song ("Kiss Me") on repeat while applying makeup and slipping into the very best little black dress I owned. I was determined to look memorable.

Fast forward to a few hours later when The Pianist is pulling me away from the crowd of friends saying that we need to go outside. I follow wordlessly. But nothing would've ever prepared me for what truly happened.

His girlfriend arrived and he wanted me to be one of the first people to meet her. I was too in shock to properly react. I numbly went through the motions of civil interaction as my heart cracked in two.

I then managed to escape the party. I didn't have a car at the time and I didn't want to tell my parents that I was abandoning the party, so I walked all the way home. And I couldn't even cry as living in a small town meant everyone knows everyone and me walking down the streets in tears would've been all over town by morning.

At home the waterfall of tears fell in painful torrents. I pulled down all the photos we had together from my wall. And then I saw it.

The cactus.

In a fit of rage I hurled it against the wall.

If you were willing to kill my love, I was willing to destroy any evidence of it.

Years later, still in love, I found myself writing a lengthy email to the Pianist. I wanted to explain my love, how I never stopped believing cause I wanted to be that radical that Ola Salo sang about so much.

You want to know what he said to my emotional vomit?

GOODLUCK.

But I guess luck has never been on my side.
If I were lucky, I never would've met you.

78

THE SOULMATE

Our love spanned several cities and many jet-lagged mornings. There were more winters than summers. Always wrapped up in bulky sweaters and coats. Our breaths rising in the cold mornings as we shared secrets and cigarettes.

Knowing you was like knowing the world. I learned everything from you. The good, the bad, and the painful. You were smart, well-read, and the right amount of cocky and charming. You were my beacon of light in the dark corridors of my heart. You illuminated everything that was good or bad about me. Maximum transparency. There was no hiding from you. I was cut open, ready for inspection like a frog that was getting dissected by a curious student.

At night we'd fall asleep curled up – exhausted. I'd fall asleep holding your guitar-callused hand feeling safe. I thought you were my soul mate, but I was young and you were reckless.

Our fights would make the walls shake with my accusations, your rage would destroy everything we had built together. You were such a confident liar and I too young and willing to believe the fables you weaved in gold to blind me of the truth.

But maybe you didn't want to see the truth either.

So we decked our eyes with stars and would live on kisses and chocolates. We whispered poetry, William Blake, Edna St. Vincent Millay, Sylvia Plath, while lying in bed our naked limbs tangled like a fishnet at rest. We lived on music and writing. Your words, my words, soon they became our words till your song and my poems were one and the same reciting the same story over and over again to audiences eager to listen to our heartbreak and love.

I'd drive fast into the night without the headlights on, using the beam of the moon as my guide in the dark. You'd hang your head out the passenger window, your black hair flying wildly in the wind and say, "We are going to live forever!" Because, forever when you are young is infinite.

We shared love, music, tears, and books. We were one.

For a moment we were soul mates.

Now you sing your stories about our love to audiences hungry with desire, and I whisper my poems to the wind because I want my words to be carried across the ocean and caress you at night when you're asleep and I'm just waking up for the day.

We were forever.

We are for never.

MY FIRST KISS

It was a typical morning in my seventh-grade life. I've never been a fan of math, especially since that year I had begun Pre-Algebra. But the only thing that made that class bearable was the fact that the boy I had a huge crush on since sixth grade sat right in front of me in class. Since we were friends, I'd often find any excuse to talk to him. I'd ask him about movies. How the Chicago Bulls were doing that season (he was a huge fan and always wore a Chicago Bulls cap, strictly backward as per the '90s cap etiquette for cool kids).

Our history was somewhat complicated. The year before I had given him a Valentine's Day card that I had made and written a poem that went along these lines:

Nobody knows of my feelings for you,
I keep them hidden, clear out of view.
But the tracks in the snow may give a clue,
But nobody knows of my love for you.

Now my grand romantic gesture would've been all fine and dandy if my best friend at the time hadn't started dating my crush that week of Valentine's. Our classes had boxes for Valentine's cards, and I had placed mine in the box on a Monday, my best friend had gotten with the said boy on a Wednesday. Valentine's fell on a Friday, so now you can see my dilemma. Drama-ensued for a while because of that, until things cleared up (hey, it's not MY fault they got together after I had posted the card!).

But back to that day in Pre-Al.

It was Halloween, my favorite holiday. All I could think about was how I was going to go Trick-Or-Treating that night (something that truly defied my social group of "pretty popular girls" cause that was seen as "childish" cause ya know when you're twelve and in a popular group, you need to act like you're fifteen). This probably explains why I ended up leaving said group, which meant also leaving behind my best friend (and also the most popular girl in seventh grade) which was social status suicide on my part, but I was a rebel!

But I digress.

I was there getting settled in my seat, trying to pretend I knew what was going on (cause ya know, I refused to wear my glasses at the time, which meant that I couldn't see a thing written on the board and I'm actually surprised I managed to earn B's in math without ever seeing how the teacher worked out the problems).

Crush Boy sat down and I was doodling on my notebook when he turned around and flashed me his usual charming smile saying, "Happy Halloween!" And then and there just kissed me.

This is where time kind of stopped for me.

My heart was hammering so hard against my chest I was certain that I was going to have a coronary right then and there. My breath caught in my throat, and my cheeks flushed in the most horrendous way (being pale sucks).

"Woo-hoo!" One guy cheered, which pulled me out of the moment and was reminded that I was still in class.

In a math class that also had my best friend (and Crush Boy's ex-girlfriend) sitting only a few rows over. I looked over in her direction, and if I weren't so near-sighted, I'm certain I could see her glaring.

Despite that kiss being simple (we were twelve and in class!), the feelings of euphoria that I experienced from it were something I chased for years, attempting so desperately to feel that lightheaded and blissful. And because this is me, no, Crush Boy and I didn't have a short-term happy ending. We never dated. Despite him always showing a strange fascination with me, but always dating other girls instead. Later that year I moved, and on my last day of school, he kissed me again (this time after our English). He came up behind me and just planted his lips on me and then said, "Good luck at your new school." I could barely murmur a reply back before he was already gone, rushing to his final class.

I never saw or heard from him after that day.
Maybe, some people are just meant to be memories.

THE ARTIST

I met you in the City of Love, or most commonly known as Paris. I was heartbroken and crying my eyes out along the Seine when you stopped me and asked me if I needed help in any way.

"Are you capable of fixing a broken heart?" I said with a slight embarrassed laugh in between the tears.

You were gentle and kind, and although your eyes are of the lightest shade of blue, they were the warmest color in that cold winter day.

You were in the city with your brother because he had a film meeting, and I was there to see *the soulmate* (brooding musician that made any girl sigh as he walked by) only to find out that what should've been a getting back together weekend turned out to be a breaking up for good when he admitted that a girl he was casually seeing was impregnated with his baby. Somehow that cemented the fact that I needed to walk away for good.

My infatuation for you was both sudden and fleeting. I loved the way you held your paintbrush as you went on a painting frenzy, mixing the colors till they transformed into magic. Your kisses were warm, but my heart was cold. I'd touch you hoping that I'd feel something inside of me stir, but my heart was too wounded to even find a weak beat in its dark crevices.

We shared cappuccinos and croissants in Florence, admired Botticelli's art, and walked along the bridge over the Arno River.

You held unto my hand as though you never wanted to let it go, and yet I always walked a step ahead of you, as though I wanted to disentangle from your affection.

And yet the months went by and I kept living in old black and white photographs whilst your world was in technicolor. You didn't know how dark my world had become, I was so good at smiling in your presence. But tears would plague me the moment I was alone. I didn't even know what I was crying over. The end of a relationship? Losing the soulmate? Or was I merely devastated that I couldn't feel what you felt for me?

Love for you was eternal Spring, whilst I was living the most dreadful winter. When it came time for me to tell you the truth and let you go, I watched your heart crack leaving dreadful red marks down your chest and I wished that I could repaint a better picture. I yearned so much that I could distort the world to make it appear as beautiful as you saw it, because I wanted so much to be a part of it, but I don't think I ever was.

The stars had abandoned me. There was only darkness in my road and you deserved the light.

THE ROMANTIC

The first time I saw you, you walked right past me and I felt my heart leap out of my chest as my gaze followed you and I said, "Who's that hot guy?"

My then-boyfriend merely laughed and told me you were a friend, and called after you. Once you returned, your eyes met mine and just like in some lame Rom-Com it felt like time had stopped for a moment, minus the cheesy pop song as the soundtrack. We spent the night drinking coffee and talking, and sometimes I'd just look over at you as you spoke animatedly with your friend.

When my phone rang, you said, "We've got the same ring tone," later showing me how you too, had the same Franz Ferdinand song. You were on my mind for days after that night. It was impossible for me to fall in love with the boy I was with, because you had eclipsed him completely. How can one love the moon, when you were the sun?

The second time we met, it was a cold December night. I had broken up with my boyfriend. Two Capricorns were never meant to be together, our stubbornness clashing in the most violent ways. We met at a coffee shop, one of the few still open at the dead of night. We drank conspicuous amounts of coffee and tried several cakes. You kept drawing me comic strips of myself. It was bliss.

Then you insisted you'd walk me back to my hotel. It was snowing. Music flowed out from a pub down the street. You grabbed me, insisted we dance. I laughed, telling you it was too cold and you pulled me to you saying, "I'll keep you warm, pretty girl."

The stars lit up your eyes, and I smiled giving in. I still was uncertain in regards to your feelings for me. But then you kissed me, and any doubts I had vanished.

Like most wonderful, charming men, you were taken. Of course, I didn't know that until *after. After* many kisses and *after* my heart was already yours. It was too late for me then to try to pull myself free of this twisted love.

You sent me so many letters after we parted. So many roses that I could've adorned a flower shop. You made me so many mix CDs filled with your own music and The Beatles, The Smashing Pumpkins, and various other artists.

The fourth time I saw you, three weeks had passed since our last encounter. But I immediately knew that something was amiss. The **THE END** was written all over your pale face by the way you grimaced when I hugged you. I knew that you were about to hit me with bad, TERRIBLE news.

I couldn't stay. I had to get away.

You kept calling me afterwards. Leaving messages, saying how we should still be friends. That we were friends before lovers.

Another month went by before I saw you again.

By then my heart was shattered. But you kept telling me how much you loved me. I was reeling on x to truly understand any of it. I only wanted to smash your heart in smithereens just as you had done with mine. I just wanted to burn anything that you had ever given to me, till there was nothing left but ashes.

"I love you," you kept repeating, like I was a child who couldn't understand. "I care very deeply for you."

I kept shaking my head. It wasn't true. It couldn't be true, or else I wouldn't feel so awful. I let go of your hand.

"Where are you going?" you said, as tears blinded me. I walked aimlessly away from you. I wanted so much to stay. But I knew I couldn't.

You were never mine for me to keep.

THE NEW YORKER

It was a hot, Coney Island summer and we were headed towards the Wonder Wheel. Hands interlocked as always, as I pulled off pieces of candy floss. The sugar melted in our mouths, sharing sticky kisses. We laughed feeling lucky for that moment. We had fallen in love in April, and although it was merely July (three months later) we felt like we had been together forever. We were inseparable. No one else mattered to us but each other. We lived on kisses and sugary sweets. We had no regard for day or night, we were always awake, always up to something.

"You know there's an old gypsy tale that if you ride the Wonder Wheel with someone else, you'll be together forever," he said to me, his dark hair blowing into his eyes.

"Are you sure you wanna be stuck with me forever?" I joked.

But I couldn't imagine my life without him. He was the one person I loved to talk to at any hour of the day, and even when we'd spend the day watching Asian horror movies and eating takeout I'd never get bored.

Like two enthusiastic kids, we got on the Wonder Wheel, feeling like we were on top of the world. Everyone below us was so tiny, and he kissed me at the top of the Ferris Wheel. I could've lived in the moment forever. I *wanted* to live in that moment forever. I wished the night would melt into my veins, and that I could swallow the stars.

"I love you," he murmured. A phrase he'd tell me so often during the day, and no matter how many times he said it still managed to make me melt. I'd wake up with him uttering his love, and drifted to sleep with him declaring it one more time. I could feel his love embrace my whole being. My heart was full. It had never felt so full before.

And then one day catastrophe struck.

Because fate is unkind to lovers. Fate tore us apart, and ever since my heart has never felt full again. Like those people who can still feel their limbs after amputation, I too, feel this phantom love. Other times I'm just aching for the part of me that isn't there because he had become so essential to my being.

I often think about that moment on the Wonder Wheel. A part of me hopes that the superstition is true. That fate can be bent and he'll find his way back to me. Or that time can be rewound and I can find myself back on the top of the Wonder Wheel, our lips sticky with sugar, sharing kisses, sharing breaths, sharing dreams.

THE SOUTHERN GENTLEMEN

We met in July. I was there to see your bestfriend perform, but after the gig you asked me if I wanted to go out for ice cream. We soon found out that the only place that serves ice cream at midnight is a Denny's Diner, so there we spent over two hours just talking about everything and anything. I loved listening to your voice. Your Texan accent was warm and inviting. We laughed like we had been friends forever.

It was perfect.

The first time you kissed me, you first stopped to kiss my nose. I smiled at the gesture. I thought that you were different. I thought that it felt nice to be in your presence. And my hand fit perfectly with your own, forever linked.

We were in Oklahoma hiding in the closet with a tornado approaching our hotel room. My heart was racing, but you held me close and strummed your guitar, singing to me, *Riders on the Storm*, as the winds increased. Tears were streaming down my cheeks. I thought our building was going to lift up just like Dorothy's home in *The Wizard of Oz*, and seeing my fear you held my hand and whispered,   "We're going to be okay. Even if this could be our final moment, I wouldn't want to be anywhere else."

We were at a gas station in the desert when your bandmates were filling up the van's tank and Van Morrison's *Brown Eyed Girl*, came on the radio. You grabbed my hand, and singing the lyrics to me, pulled me out of the van. I laughed as we danced under the hot desert sun. Your crooked smile made me melt, and once again I thought that everything about that moment, about us, was perfect.

And for a while it truly was.

Until.

This is the part in the story where it takes a detour for the worst.

Until you grew weary of me wanting more. Needing more. And it crushed my heart when you handed me a ring for my birthday but punctuated, "It's not the sort of ring you were hoping for, you know I'm not ready, *yet*."

But that *yet* kept weighing on me. Was it really a yet, or were you just buying time? I began to believe that you didn't care. I was certain that you were getting bored or maybe exhausted of me.

Then one February night, I saw my phone with all your texts and voicemails. You had spent most of the day trying to reach me because you were going to break up with me. Something deep inside of me broke. And like Thom Yorke in *Karma Police*, for a minute there I *did* lose myself. I spent my nights driving around L.A. listening to songs on repeat as I tried to find a way to get back to you. I'd text you obsessively. Sometimes I was sweet, other times I was angry. I reached a point where I didn't care whether the attention I was receiving from you was positive or negative. I was starving for any tiny morsel. Your hate would've been better to me than your indifference. And all I could think about was how much I missed you. I started to hate you because I didn't like this new person I had become. But at the same time, I didn't know how to be different. I spent two years trying to forget the twenty months we spent together.

You hollowed me out. Sometimes, I feel as though if anyone peers closely into me they can see just how much I'm lacking. That they can see how all my cracks haven't been placed correctly, that I'm not fixed. And maybe I never will be.

This is the new me. Not newly minted, but an amalgam of broken pieces haphazardly glued together, trying to pretend that I'm okay.

I'm okay.

I hope that wherever you are, you're okay too.

THE BROODING BOY

You were like November rain on a summer day, bringing storm clouds into the room.

I was wearing a pink shirt the day we met. I wanted to seem innocuous, nice. Someone others could depend on. Most of all, I just wanted your mother to hire me. And she did. But you resented the fact that I was six months younger than you and had already graduated from high school. You hated that your mother put me in charge of taking care of the dogs because she knew that you were too busy brooding and hating life to remember.

You had a natural disdain towards me, as you'd walk into the home, headphones on and a scowl on your face. You almost seethed the time I suggested you wear primer if you were going to use eyeliner and black eye shadow. "It won't get so messy," I said.

You glared at me and replied, "I am a mess."

Several weeks went by, where I'd take care of the pups and you'd head straight to your room, ignoring me. Until one day when you came out of your room crying. Black tears rushed down your cheeks and I knew it was serious when I asked you what was wrong and all you could manage to say was, "My fucking dad."

And then I knew that you had been lying all those times you said you didn't care about him, because why else would you cry for a man who couldn't make the time to come and see you as he had promised to?

"I'm sorry," I whispered because I wasn't sure how to comfort a grown boy who was jagged glass covered in tears. So I made you cookies and we played Doom 3, because who doesn't feel better after sugar and (virtually) shooting?

After that fateful afternoon there was a sudden shift in our interactions. You no longer saw me as an annoying gnat and instead of staying locked up in your room you'd come along whenever I'd take the pups for a walk. Sometimes you'd even drive us to the 7-Eleven for blue raspberry slushies and strawberry Twizzlers, our tongues a vibrant blue as we laughed over dumb jokes. I was too young to be bold (I know it's unfathomable for anyone to believe me, because you only have known me now). Or maybe I was smart enough to know that it's never wise to makeout with your employer's son. So I never did. *But oh did I want to.*

I'd spend all day at the restaurant hotel waiting tables and running daydreams through my head of all the possibilities that could involve you and counting down the hours 'til was 4 o'clock and I could rush to your house. This was the era of MySpace and I had printed all the photos of you and taped them in my diary adorning them with Placebo lyrics, cause *Dreams of a face that is pure perfection,* seemed like they had been written for you. It didn't matter that your front teeth were crooked and you had rogue zits. I was in love and felt like anything was possible, although really, that was merely a far-fetched dream.

You were in a band with some of your friends and you called yourselves Everlasting Fire. I'd sing your songs and almost burst with happiness when you listed me as your Top Friend on MySpace. We spent ten months together, where we shared anything and everything. I didn't feel silly telling you that I wanted to be an actress, cause you actually believed that I'd become one. When your school had a Spring Fair, you invited me along. You bought me cotton candy and when we rode on the carousel you leaned over and kissed me. It tasted like spun sugar and crashing stars. And I wanted that moment to last *forever*.

Then one day, months after your high school graduation, you came home radically different. You had cut your long black hair, wiped off all of your eye makeup, and informed me that you'd be leaving for boot camp soon.

"But what about UCLA?" I could feel my heart cracking with every word.

"I changed my mind. I need to get out of L.A. Make a difference."

I was upset. So upset that I told your mom that I had to quit. That I was picking up night shifts at the hotel and couldn't look after the pups anymore. I simply couldn't remain in a home that breathed your name without you being there.

And for years I didn't think about you. It was easier that way. Until recently. When you came in my dream. You were always a sneaky asshole.

In the dream, we were at your high school's gym. Your hair was still long, your bright ocean eyes still rimmed in black. You were seated on the bleachers and I was walking by. Fast. And you said, "Hey, why are you in such a hurry?"

For some reason, the gym was dressed like a gaudy Christmas tree, lights, and garlands. Streamers everywhere. It seemed like it were ready for a dance, only we were alone in that darkened room. And I told you, "I can't stay. It's too late."

…...and you came down from the bleachers, tugged on my hand but I walked away.

You don't know this, but now I am the November rain on a summer day.

See how far I've come?

A ROAD MAP IN MUSIC

Scar Tissue – Red Hot Chili Peppers
I'll make it to the moon if I have to crawl....

We were thirteen and wide-eyed with curiosity. We'd spend those lazy summer days going to the pool or the beach, trying our best to look like swimsuit models. Drinking way too many coffees and smoking in her bedroom with the windows wide open letting the August heat drape over our bodies, glowing with sweat, because you don't know what living in a furnace is like until you've spent a summer in Sicily. We'd thumb through beauty magazines, and talk about how we'd live in cooler cities when we were older, like Los Angeles, Paris, maybe even London. That we'd get rock star boyfriends with swoon-worthy accents and crooked smiles who'd write songs about us. We were only thirteen so you should forgive our naivety. The thing is, it's not that fairytales don't exist, it's that only some people get a happy ending. It breaks my heart that she never got hers. It breaks my heart that on a Christmas Eve she couldn't find a reason to stay alive.

K – Cigarettes After Sex
I remember when I first noticed when you liked me back....

My limbs were like jelly, and I couldn't tell if it was because of the x we had taken, or simply because he had that effect on me. The stars that night looked like explosions in the sky, so bright and destructive. I know Cher made a whole movie about being moonstruck, but what about a passion that bursts like asteroids? The moon is steady in its rotation, there are no jerky movements, no irregular jumps. But we were like crashing stars, unable to control our paths, unable to deviate me from crashing into him. It was inevitable. It was dangerous. But my blood was filled with adrenaline, and I didn't think of the consequences. I could only think about his lips and the fire in each kiss. I'd trace, I love you, on his skin with my fingers cause I couldn't utter the words. Because those words held a weight that could make the whole world implode. So I'd just lie back, and stare up at the sky, hoping that the stars could somehow spell out my future. Or maybe we could just get hit by an asteroid and burn together.

Speed of Pain – Marilyn Manson
I want to outrace the speed of pain....

It was one of those nights where the sky fell apart and the darkness had descended its thick blanket over the entire city. Specifically, me. All I could think about were all the ways my heart had been broken, and how I couldn't seem to fit the pieces back together. And did it really matter? That's the thing about broken hearts. They never recover. They always remain damaged, with a weak beat, no matter how much glue I could slap on all the cracks and crevices. And then, because I was twenty and drunk on lovelorn promises, I did the only reasonably stupid thing people do in those circumstances, swallowed as many pills as I could possibly manage, cause I hadn't been sleeping in days, and I figured that a deep sleep would cure all my sadness. It's telling when you keep your emotions so guarded, that you're always the joking-fun friend, that the one time you send a serious text to a friend, they come running knowing that something must be fatally *wrong*. And some days, it crosses my mind that the only difference between Marilyn Monroe and me is that I just had a friend who raced across the city so that he could make me vomit.

Venice Bitch – Lana Del Rey
Paint me happy and blue....

I was drowning in the blue of his eyes, I knew the waters below us were like ice. And yet, with eyes closed, I kept leaning closer towards the edge of the Ferris Wheel. The wind slapping against our faces, and I reached out for his hand. I was certain that if I didn't grab it in time, I was sure to fall off. To slip away right into the deep blue waters. There were so many words on the tip of my tongue, so many promises that I wanted to say but I couldn't navigate through the messiness of emotions. Because when my heart is beating so hard I can feel it in my throat, all I can utter are breathless affirmations. Everyone below us seemed so damn happy, and I wanted to promise you that same happiness. But how can someone so full of cracks be able to promise something so pristine? How can someone sell a dream of something they've never held and understood? So I just held on tighter, thinking that would be the only way that I wouldn't fall into the void.

DREAM LOVER

It always begins in the same way.

I'm walking down the cracked earth barefoot, my long red chiffon dress flows behind me. The sun is setting and the sky is an explosion of purples and pinks like some strange Dali painting. The trees lining the path are gnarled and twisted with little sad tufts that are never going to bloom into anything spectacular. The rocky path should cut my feet, and maybe it does, but I never seem to feel it.

I never see him whole, but little parts like he's a mystery I need to solve. Like the tip of a black leather shoe peaking from behind a tree, or the blonde hair that barely touches the black jacket, a stark contrast between light and dark.

The rugged rock formations look both eerie and majestic once the fog settles in, and the crows circle the sky like they're waiting for some strange kind of omen to materialize. I walk closer, so close that I could almost touch his shoulder if I were to reach my hand out.

But I don't.

It's not because I am afraid.

But.

Maybe.

Because I know that if I see his eyes, then I will melt and become one with the sky. My skin and bones will become little tapestries strewn across the clouds.

When I wake from those dreams, I'm often left with this strange sinking feeling that needs to be quickly removed.

And so I kiss him awake till he's pulled out of sleep, till he's unable to resist and he murmurs my name like it's a curse or a prayer. Maybe it's both. Soon we're a tangle of limbs and whispered words until I'm slowly spreading my legs and my nails claim his skin just as his tongue claims my body. And in those fleeting moments, I could swear that the walls around us fall, and I'm in that same barren place with the twisted trees and cactus, and if I look up at the ceiling I can see that same vivid purple skies that bleed various hues of pinks and orange.

Then he whispers, "Mine," his lips against the inside of my thigh.

"Yours," I reply, but my voice is merely a gasp, my head still spinning and my heart on the verge of breaking free from my ribcage.

BURN BABY BURN

I smelled the smoke before I saw the flames. It was intoxicating and made me feel woozy, and I thought, *Not again.* I rushed down the hallway, heart in my throat when I felt the heat from the flames. They seemed to dance seductively like one of those skimpy-clothed belly dancers swaying and casting their spell on you.

I closed my eyes, basking in the heat. I should've been alarmed, but as the flames drew closer I remained oddly calm. When I opened my eyes again I saw that the roof had burned down and I watched with mild fascination at the night sky.

When he came up to me he asked, "Why did you do it?"

At first, I didn't understand his question, but when I looked down I saw that I was still clutching the matches in my hands. Then I understood. But instead of looking back at him I simply gazed up at the sky and replied, "I just wanted to see the stars."

A MAN

A man. I was told he was difficult by women who had tried sleeping with him. I was new in the city, and he was friendly. He suggested we hang out, and I wanted to see why all the girls adored him. For someone who had the reputation of being difficult, he was too eager to get me naked. He was also the sort of dude to get amnesia and tried to act like we never fucked. Too bad I didn't care.

A man. It was raining in London. I was there for a photoshoot. He was there shooting a movie. He had a charming way about him, and he knew that. We went drinking and then he said we should go back to his hotel room, where he pushed me against the wall and whispered in my ear, "Do you like being fucked hard and dirty?" Then he slut-shamed me with his friends. Cause ya know, *boys will be boys.*

A man. I know he had a darkness buried deep inside of him. I wanted to lift it out, make it my own. A part of me was afraid that he might forget about me, or that he might think I was too crazy, too wild. Just *too much.* But I wanted him to fall in love with me, because a part of me was already in love with him. "Don't leave, please stay with me tonight," I whispered to him after giving him a blowjob. I wanted to tear my heart out and let him slip inside.

A man. A former co-worker that I used to have a crush on. A part of me always knew that he liked me. We drank whiskey and he confessed, "I thought about eating your pussy. I used to jerk off thinking about it." I suppose a guy with a crooked smile can get away with using that as a pick-up line.

A man. We were friends, and he asked me to see him after the Academy Awards viewing party I had attended. Free booze always has me drinking way more champagne and cocktails than I should, and I arrived at his house feeling bold. Torn fabric and runaway crystals skidded across the floor. This is how you destroy a dress.

A man. I tried to push a candle through his darkness, but he was always pulling away. I've always appreciated those who can be unafraid. He wasn't one of them.

A man. We had worked together before. He was much older than me. New York. I stripped for him as he smoked a joint. I knew he had a darkness in him that could sometimes consume him. I wanted that darkness to consume me. He wrote me poems that seeped with desire. I loved him like an addict needing their next hit. Until there was nothing left of us except for blood and bone.

A man. Sometimes he'd say he liked me. Most of the time he didn't. Probably, all the time to be honest. He despised my collection of never-ending men. But I was greedy. I wanted them all. Like a kleptomaniac stealing pieces from every person.

A man. He was beautiful and easily forgiving of my mistakes. I was careless and would pout like a child. Tea dates around London and flowers. He thought I was a Lolita. But I'm a Marla Singer ready to tear your heart.

THE LONGING

For days I'd absently touch my lips trying to jolt the memory of your kiss. Why had it been different than the others? I needed to pinpoint the *why* as though that could possibly offer me some answers. I'd scan through messages on my phone, always hoping to see yours there among the many that I only glossed over with bored, manufactured replies. My mind kept replaying how it felt to have your head between my legs and hoping that my taste lingered on your tongue for days.

My heart was in love far longer than *I* ever wanted to admit that I was. I didn't want to fall in love again or be in a relationship. I was still plagued by dreams of my last encounter with my ex, where I walked in the snow for hours in New York City as my charming ex followed me in his car with the passenger window rolled down, flashing me his Dorian Gray smile while leaning across the seat and saying, "Come on, get in. Everything's going to be okay."

But I kept on stubbornly walking, tears streaming down my cheeks as they left scalding imprints.

"This is the end, because things are only ever okay at the end."

He looked at me like I had delivered him the wrong line and wasn't sure what his cue was. Maybe that's why he first replied with a nervous laugh and then seeing the error of his ways, tried to remedy with, "I beg you, get in. Please. You're going to get sick."

I glared back at him to show that his charm wouldn't win me over this time as it had done so many other times in the past. That I had grown tedious of his inability to see how we were only hurting one another.

"Who cares? I'm already sick," I yelled back. "I'm sick of you. And me. Together."

Sometimes brutal honesty is misconstrued as cruelty.

He thought I didn't really mean it.

I did.

I don't know why I wanted more from you, but I guess I couldn't stay away from the kisses and the feeling of safety that was found within the warmth of your arms. But I'm glad I stuck around, although missing you when you're across the globe from me can suck like hell.

THE VOID

We stared up at the sky and the stars were swimming along the darkness of the night. Like a Van Gogh painting in motion, the colors melted into one canvas. I was so moved I wanted to sing *Vincent*, but the lyrics were escaping me and all I could grasp onto was the melody and I hummed it under my breath.

Sweat trickled down my back and the infernal heat of that Spanish summer didn't seem to cease as I closed my eyes and clung to the rugged rocks and patchy grass. But everything was in motion, although I was lying still. Perhaps the rum that had consumed was to blame, or maybe the yellow chalky pill engraved with a smiley face and a promise of, "It'll make you smile," as it melted on my tongue was the real culprit.

"The sky is gonna fall and it's going to swallow me," I said to you.

You just laughed at me and said, "If it's falling then it would crush you, not swallow you."

And I replied, "No, the sky is a dragon."

All the while I kept my eyes closed because I could feel the tears itching to fall. Instead, I got up on my wobbly feet, walking towards the edge of the cliff. I could hear the waves crashing beneath, not furious but steady.

"Where you going?" you shouted.

"I need....the water...." but I don't even remember if I had told you or I merely said it to myself because you shouted again.

"Hey! Don't! It's dark!" And I heard you stand.

I opened my eyes and ran, and didn't stop till I leaped into the void. It all happened so fast. And for a fleeting moment I felt like I was flying. For a moment I felt like the stars were gonna reach down and scoop me up from the fall.

But they didn't.

And I fell into the sea beneath me. The water drowned out your shouts from above and all I could think while engulfed in the that dark vacuum was, *Is it this easy to die at twenty-three, and why didn't you jump after me?*

Maybe I scared you, because I wasn't scared myself.

STRAWBERRY FIELDS FOREVER

My feet dangle in mid-air as I sit on a windowsill in my apartment in New York. *It's dangerous*, I can hear my mom's voice weave it's way into my head as a warning. But I love the feeling of nothingness beneath me. I'm eating Swiss chocolates as I stare out into the city skyline. Aluminum foils from the chocolate wrappers littered behind me, twinkling like stars. We're like angels, we have wings in our muscles.

The bath water reeks of strawberries, as they float around me like suspended hearts. I watch them bob, as the water turns to a faint shade of red.

"What are you going to do with $200 worth of strawberries?" the salesclerk had asked. "Having a party?"

T. Rex is gliding from the vinyl and exploding into my room in mirages of glitter and feather boas.

"No one falls in love nowadays," my stylist told me as he fluffed out my hair, "Love is a disorder of the heart."

I'm crushing the strawberries with my hands. Little hearts that bleed into the water. *Kiss me, my psychopath.* Share my disease.

Rivers of champagne, clothes strewn across the floor.

"I heard you like the bad girls honey, is that true?" moans Lana.

I'm vomiting emotions on your carpet. I don't know how to do romance right. My heart is like a supernova, and it's exploding into a million pieces. Your hands are getting bloody from trying to gather up the fragments. Bruises are the side-effect of passion. I can fly like an angel, I've got wings on my back.

Los Angeles. We're sitting on the kitchen floor. I'm blowing bubbles. On my phone unread messages and missed calls. Glasses filled with various drinks. The scent of green tea takes me back in time. Sticky, summer nights where the air felt heavy. Thick as honey.

I was singing, "See you at the bitter end," as fireflies danced along the lake. My past is an echo sliced in two.

He touches my hand, and it's like a symphony. *Fantaisie Impromtu.* I'm going to go live on the Eiffel Tower, and dangle my legs into nothingness. Launching strawberries from my room, and they'll explode upon impact, like a supernova, bloody stars. We're like angels. We've got wings on our backs.

The rest of the ride, is riding on you.

THE DAY THAT ROMANCE DIED

Maybe, on an idle day, when everything is calm and the breeze is sweet, out of the blue you'll be reminded of me.

Unexpectedly.

Like most things that aren't pleasant, it will hit you.

And it will ache like a sharp knife nestled in the center of your chest.

Maybe then you'll understand the mad poets, the fools who'll give up anything for a kiss.

Maybe at that moment you'll realize how much carelessness and egoism severs ties and tarnishes loyalty.

Or maybe not.

Maybe everything will just become a box of faded photographs with trinkets that hold no sentimental value anymore.

A love that flees, rarely returns, because a love that flees never wanted to stay. And I'll just be viewed as a mistake, a minor lapse of judgment, for a story that started with a kiss has ended in massacre.

Oh, let's have a party for all the mess we made.

Maybe romanticism isn't dead, but I wouldn't know it. One night I told my heart to go fuck itself and I haven't seen it since.

Dear Reader,

Thank you very much for reading my poetry and prose collection, *Lost Girls Go Everywhere.*
If you enjoyed it, I'd greatly appreciate it if you would take a moment to rate it on Amazon and/or Goodreads. And if you have the time, a review – no matter the length – will help new readers decide if this poetry and prose collection is for them as well as provide me with valuable feedback.

Thank you, and see you on the dark side.

Best,

Azzurra

Goodreads:
https://www.goodreads.com/author/show/12633660.Azzurra_Nox
Official Website: http://azzurranox.com/
Twitter: @diva_zura
Instagram: @divazura
Blog: https://theinkblotters.com/
Contact: azzurranox@yahoo.com

Also by Azzurra Nox

CUT HERE

Doll Parts: Tales of Twisted Love

My American Nightmare – Women in Horror
Anthology Vol. 1

Strange Girls – Women in Horror Anthology Vol. 2

Bleed Like Me: Poems for the Broken

"Good Sister, Bad Sister" in Betty Bites Back:
Stories to Scare the Patriarchy

"Baby Teeth" in Midnight in the Pentagram

ABOUT THE AUTHOR

Azzurra Nox was born in Catania, Sicily and has led a nomadic life since birth. She has lived in various European cities and Cuba and currently resides in So-Cal. Her love for the macabre began at a young age when she discovered horror movies. Her writing draws inspiration from music, literature, and her nightmares. Her latest project was STRANGE GIRLS – WOMEN IN HORROR ANTHOLOGY, in which she was an editor and contributing writer for. She curates a lifestyle blog, The Inkblotters (www.theinkblotters.com) where she shares her love for books, beauty products, films, music, and events. When she isn't writing, she loves dancing, going to rock shows, spending time with her fiance, and cuddling her two chubby rescue pups, Nico and Lupo.